Come Home, Angus

BY **Patrick Downes**

ILLUSTRATIONS BY **Boris Kulikov**

ORCHARD BOOKS • NEW YORK • AN IMPRINT OF SCHOLASTIC INC.

LIBRARY OF CONGRESS CATALOGING-IN-PUBLICATION DATA

Downes, Patrick, 1968– author.
Come home, Angus / by Patrick Downes ; illustrated by Boris Kulikov. — First edition.   pages   cm
Summary: Little Angus wakes up angry and decides to run away from home when his mother scolds him for
being rude—but he is very soon lost, hungry, and more than a little frightened.
ISBN 978-0-545-59768-5
1. Runaway children—Juvenile fiction. 2. Mothers and sons—Juvenile fiction. 3. Anger in children—Juvenile fiction.
[1. Runaways—Fiction. 2. Mothers and sons—Fiction. 3. Anger—Fiction.] I. Kulikov, Boris, 1966- illustrator. II. Title.
PZ7.1.D687Co 2016   [E]—dc23   2015027228

10 9 8 7 6 5 4 3 2 1   16 17 18 19 20

Printed in Malaysia   108 • First edition, August 2016

Boris's paintings are created in a mixed-media style including an acrylic wash, graphite pencil, pen, ink, and oil pastels.
On some of the paintings, to increase the color intensity, Boris uses a black tea wash.
The text type was set in Hoefler TextRoman. The display type was set in Bawdy Bold. Book design by Marijka Kostiw

For my mother and for Michèle — P.D.

For Andre, Max, and Kate — B.K.

Angus woke up angry.

He didn't know why; he just did.

Clive, his dachshund, annoyed him when they walked:

"You're too slow."

His canary, Pennycake,

drove him crazy with her singing:

"You're too loud."

"Stop all that purring,"

Angus ordered Arthur, his cat.

When Angus sat down to breakfast, he refused to eat:

"These pancakes are skinny."

"Look who's in a bad mood," Angus's mother said.
"I heard you yell at Clive, scold Pennycake, and
shout at Arthur. You didn't eat your breakfast.
That's no way to behave. You'll have to apologize."

Angus frowned. Angus growled. Angus held his head.

"Mama!" he yelled. "Mama, I don't have to listen to you. I'm mad. I'm madder than mad. I don't have to be nice."

"Oh-yes-you-do," Angus's mother said. "In this house, being angry doesn't let you be rude."

"Then," Angus said, "I won't live here anymore."

He went to his room and found his backpack. He shoved in a pair of underwear and a pair of socks. He pushed in a book.

In the kitchen, he found a flashlight, and he made it fit.

Oh, one more thing.

He returned to his room

for his stuffed gorilla, Snoo.

"You're really going?" his mother said.

"Yes." Angus put on his backpack.

"I'll miss you."

"No, you won't," Angus said, and left.

Angus walked a block.

He walked two blocks.

He walked three

and four and five blocks

before he stopped.

Nothing looked familiar. Only stores; no houses. The streets were busier, noisier, wider, darker. He had walked farther than he had ever walked on his own.

He had walked into a whole new world.

Angus was afraid.

He sat down on a bench and took off his pack. He opened it to get out his sardine sandwich. Sardines would make him feel better, but there was no sandwich. Angus had forgotten food.

A man strolled by with his dog.

The man waved and the dog wagged,

but Angus didn't know them.

A woman sat next to Angus with her lunch. He didn't know her either, but she smiled with her mouth full.

More strangers walked to and fro, to and fro, fast, fast, fast.

Angus had enough. He couldn't wait to see Clive, Pennycake, and Arthur. He couldn't wait to see his mother.

Angus put on his pack.

"Angus, honey, are you ready to come home?"

He turned around.

There she stood, his mother, leaning against
a lamppost.

Angus nodded.

"I'm so glad," she said.

Then she held out a small paper bag.

"Sardine sandwich?"

The bread was mushy,

wheat not white, but Angus

ate and ate.